The Pony-Mad Princess

A Puzzle for Princess Ellie

Diana Kimpton

Illustrated by Lizzie Finlay

USBORNE

For Liam

First published in 2004 by Usborne Publishing Ltd., Usborne House,
83-85 Saffron Hill, London EC1N 8RT, England. www.usborne.com

Based on an original concept by Anne Finnis.

A CIP catalogue record for this book is available from the British Library.

ISBN 0 7460 6020 3

Printed in Great Britain.

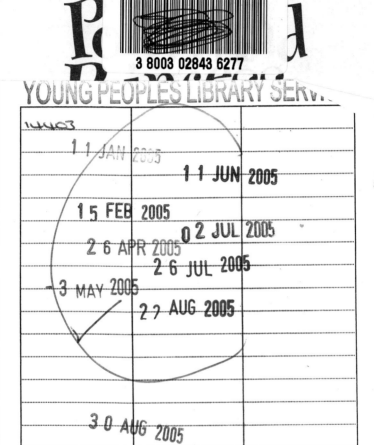
 **CUMBRIA LIBRARY SERVICES**

COUNTY COUNCIL
This book is due to be returned on or before the last date above. It
may be renewed by personal application, post or telephone, if not in
demand.

C.L.18

Look out for more sparkly adventures of
The Pony-Mad Princess!

Princess Ellie to the Rescue

Princess Ellie's Secret

Princess Ellie's Starlight Adventure

Princess Ellie's Moonlight Mystery

A Surprise for Princess Ellie

Chapter 1

"Let's explore," said Princess Ellie, as she stopped Rainbow at the entrance to the wood. The path through it was like a long, dark tunnel. On one side was a high brick wall. On the other were trees growing so close together that their branches arched overhead and shut out the sun.

"Are you sure?" said her best friend,

Kate. The palomino she was riding fidgeted from foot to foot, her golden coat gleaming in the sunshine. Moonbeam was the most nervous of Ellie's four ponies.

"Yes," said Ellie, firmly. She wasn't ready to go back to the palace yet. When she was there, she had to be Aurelia, not Ellie. She had to follow rules and behave like a proper princess. Out here she was free to do as she liked.

Ellie squeezed with her legs and Rainbow stepped forward obediently with her ears pricked. Kate followed close behind on Moonbeam.

"It's spooky in here," said Kate nervously, as they rode into the shade of the trees.

A Puzzle for Princess Ellie

"Don't be silly," laughed Ellie. "Surely you don't believe in ghosts." Riding Rainbow gave her confidence. The grey pony was so brave and reliable.

It was very quiet in the wood. There were no birds singing, and the path was covered with a thick, springy layer of rotting leaves that deadened the sound of the ponies' hooves.

As they rode deeper and deeper into the wood, Ellie looked round at the moss-covered wall and the damp tree trunks. "Kate's right," she thought. "It is a bit spooky in here." She pushed the grey pony into a trot, eager to reach the sunshine on the other side as quickly as possible.

Rainbow seemed uneasy too. She tucked in her head and blew down her nose nervously.

Suddenly, Rainbow stopped. Ellie was taken completely by surprise and shot forward out of the saddle. Rainbow didn't give Ellie time to recover her balance. Instead, the grey pony whirled around on the spot, trying to head back the way they had come.

Ellie swung sideways. She felt herself falling and tried to grab hold of the saddle. But she had already gone too far. With a sickening thud, she landed flat on her back on the ground, clutching the reins tightly in one hand.

"Are you all right?" asked Kate, anxiously.

A Puzzle for Princess Ellie

Ellie wasn't sure. She lay motionless for a moment, shocked by the force of her landing. Then, she warily moved her arms and legs a little. To her relief, there was no pain. Nothing was broken. Only her pride was damaged. "I think so," Ellie finally replied, as she climbed slowly to her feet. She brushed the dirt from her pale pink jodhpurs and straightened the pink and gold silk cover on her hard hat.

Kate looked relieved. "I think Rainbow would be back at the stables by now if you hadn't kept hold of the reins."

"Steady, girl," soothed Ellie, as she walked up to the tense, uneasy pony and stroked her neck. "There's nothing to be scared of."

Rainbow relaxed at the sound of her voice and rubbed her head gently on Ellie's shoulder.

"Shall we go back?" said Kate. "We don't want another accident."

"No," said Ellie. "I think she's all right now, and all my books say you should never let a pony win." She put her foot in the stirrup and mounted quickly. As soon as Rainbow felt her weight in the saddle, she started edging back the way they had come.

"It's not time to go home yet," said Ellie, firmly. She turned the pony to face the spot where she had fallen off. This time she was ready for trouble.

Rainbow walked forward reluctantly,

glancing from side to side and snorting through her nose. Then, at exactly the same place as before, she suddenly stopped again.

This time Ellie didn't lose her balance. But she was still shaken. What on earth was wrong with Rainbow? She had never acted like this before. "Go on, girl," Ellie called encouragingly, as she pushed the pony on with her legs. Her voice sounded extra loud in the stillness of the wood.

Rainbow didn't go on. Instead, she whirled around to the left. Ellie wasn't quick enough to stop her so she made Rainbow keep turning until she was back where she had started. Then she tried to make her walk on again.

But Rainbow took a step backwards and then whirled suddenly to the right. Ellie's heart was pounding as she struggled to stay in the saddle.

"I'll try going in front," said Kate. "Maybe Rainbow will follow us." But Moonbeam refused to go past the grey mare. She just stood still and wouldn't move.

"What's wrong with them?" said Ellie. "There's nothing there."

"Nothing we can see anyway," said Kate.

Ellie felt a thrill of excitement mixed with fear. "I just remembered something," she said. "Some people believe horses can see ghosts."

Kate looked around nervously. "I told you it was spooky."

Ellie peered along the shadowy path ahead. Was there really something there – something only Rainbow could see?

Chapter 2

"Are you going to try again?" asked Kate.

"I don't know," said Ellie. "Suppose there is something there…" Her voice trailed away. Was she being silly? Was she worrying about nothing?

Kate glanced at her watch. "We should be getting back," she said, hopefully. "Gran will be cross if I'm late."

"No, she won't," laughed Ellie. Kate's gran was the palace cook and she was never cross. "But my parents will be." For once Ellie was pleased that the King and Queen were so strict about mealtimes. It gave her and Kate an excuse to leave this spooky wood.

The two girls turned their ponies back the way they had come. It was a relief to canter out into the sunshine. After one last glance at the dark woods, they headed home to the palace.

By the time they were back at the stables, Ellie felt much calmer. From that safe distance, the idea of a haunted wood seemed more exciting than frightening. "Do you think it really was a ghost?" she asked Kate, as they filled the water buckets.

A Puzzle for Princess Ellie

"It must have been," Kate replied. "It's the only possible explanation."

Ellie bit her lip thoughtfully as she moved the hose from a full bucket to an empty one. "But I thought ghosts prowled corridors and slid through walls. What's one doing in a wood?"

Kate laughed. "Maybe one of your ancestors liked growing trees." She waved her hands above her head and said in a spooky voice, "Ooooh! I'm Archduke Edgar, the ghostly gardener. And I'm coming to get you."

As Kate ran towards her, Ellie sprayed her with the hose. Kate squealed, grabbed the hose and sprayed her back.

The water fight lasted until it was broken up by Meg, the palace groom. By then, both girls were dripping wet and giggling.

"I don't know what's got into you two today," said Meg. "You'd better go home and get dry."

*

A Puzzle for Princess Ellie

As Ellie ran up the stairs to her very pink bedroom, she couldn't stop thinking about the mystery in the wood. Was it really a ghostly gardener, or could it be something more menacing? It was a real puzzle and Ellie was determined to solve it. She decided to start by asking her governess. Miss Stringle had a passion for royal history. She was sure to know if anything weird had ever happened in that wood.

With her plan in mind, Ellie bounced into the schoolroom the next morning full of enthusiasm. Her heart sank as she saw the selection of strange-shaped spoons laid out on Miss Stringle's desk.

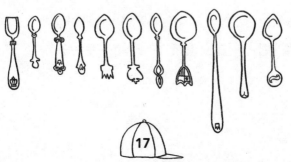

The Pony-Mad Princess

It was a test on table manners and she had completely forgotten to do her revision.

The soup spoon was easy to identify. So was the extra long one for ice-cream sundaes because she used one so often. The others had her completely stumped.

"No, no, no," said Miss Stringle in exasperation, as Ellie made yet another wild guess. "Please concentrate, Princess Aurelia."

Ellie cringed. She hated her real name almost as much as she hated this test.

Miss Stringle waved the source of Ellie's latest mistake. "This spoon is not for pickled onions. It is only for eating caviar from coddled eggs."

A Puzzle for Princess Ellie

Ellie felt tears fill her eyes. Concentrating wouldn't make any difference. She just didn't know the answers. She wished all the spoons would disappear in a puff of smoke.

They didn't. Instead, the schoolroom door burst open and in swept the King and Queen. They both looked a little flustered.

Miss Stringle curtseyed deeply. "Is there anything wrong, Your Majesties?"

"The Emperor and Empress of Andirovia are arriving this afternoon on a state visit," said the Queen.

"I know that already," said Ellie. The whole palace had been in turmoil for days, as an army of servants scrubbed and cleaned in preparation for the great event.

"But we've only just found out that

they're bringing their son," continued
the Queen.

"Prince John's the same age as you,"
said the King. "And he's sure to be bored
while we conduct our official business
with his parents. So we've decided you
must entertain him for the whole week."

"It will be fun for you to have a friend,"
added the Queen.

"I have a friend already," said Ellie,
firmly. She wasn't sure she wanted
another one, especially a boy.

"But Kate's not a princess," said Miss
Stringle. "It would be so much better
to have a royal friend."

Ellie glowered at her. She hated to
hear Kate criticized just because her gran
was a cook instead of a queen.

A Puzzle for Princess Ellie

"Of course, you won't be able to have lessons while he's here," said the King, with a smile.

Ellie brightened up immediately. A whole week with no school would be brilliant. It would be worth putting up with having a boy around if it meant not having homework. "Can I stop now?" she asked, with what she hoped would be a last glance at the dreaded spoons.

The Queen laughed. "Of course, you can, Aurelia. It will give you plenty of time for a last ride." As she turned to leave, she added, "Our visitors are arriving at five. Please wear your ermine."

Ellie stared at her in disbelief. "What do you mean – last ride?" she asked.

"Surely that's obvious," said the Queen.

The Pony-Mad Princess

"It's your duty to keep Prince John happy," explained the King. "That will take all your time so, while he is here, there is to be absolutely no riding, no playing with ponies, and no sneaking off to spend time at the stables."

Chapter 3

Ellie was horrified, but she knew there was no point in arguing. Once her parents started talking about duty, she could never change their minds. Duty was the downside of being a princess. So was wearing pink, having waving lessons, and taking dreadful tests about spoons. The upside was having four ponies.

She spent the rest of the day with them, filling her mind with sights and smells to carry her through the pony-less week ahead. First, she took Shadow, the Shetland, for a drive through the deer park in his carriage. Then, Meg gave her a jumping lesson on Sundance and, after lunch, Ellie explored the banks of the stream on Moonbeam. She was so busy that she stopped puzzling over the mystery in the wood.

The hours went by too quickly – much faster than they would have done in school. Before she had a chance to ride Rainbow, it was time for Ellie to get ready to welcome the royal visitors. She walked sadly round the yard giving each pony a last pat and promising to be back as soon as she could. Then she reluctantly returned to the palace.

A Puzzle for Princess Ellie

The royal hairdresser was waiting for Ellie in her bedroom. He tugged at her unruly curls with a comb, while she sat on a pink velvet chair and stared dismally into the pink-edged mirror.

"Dearie me," said the hairdresser, wrinkling his nose in disgust. He pulled a piece of straw from her hair and held it out at arm's length as if it might bite.

"What has Your Royal Highness been doing?"

"Having fun," said Ellie, miserably. She didn't feel like talking. She was already missing her ponies and it was only a few minutes since she last saw them.

The Pony-Mad Princess

An hour later, Ellie met her parents at the grand entrance to the palace. She was cleaner and smarter, but no happier. Her curls had been bullied into ringlets and tied with pink bows. Her silver sandals were trimmed with crystal beads and her long pink velvet dress had ermine around the hem of its full skirt. The ermine was fake. Even duty couldn't persuade Ellie to wear real fur from dead animals.

"You look beautiful, Aurelia," said the Queen, as she straightened the tiara on Ellie's head. She was wearing her best crown and positively dripping in diamonds.

The King peered towards the palace gates. "They're coming," he announced. "I can see their car." He tugged at the jacket of his red uniform to make sure it was straight, and adjusted the angle of his plumed hat.

Ellie followed her parents down the wide, stone steps as a limousine swept up to the entrance and pulled to a halt in front of them. A footman opened the rear door and out stepped the royal visitors.

The Emperor came first, dressed in naval uniform with an impressive row of medals.

The Pony-Mad Princess

Ellie wondered if he was really as fierce as he looked. The beard that covered the bottom half of his face made it hard to see if he was smiling.

The Empress looked much friendlier. She smiled warmly at Ellie. "You must be Princess

Aurelia," she said, as she kissed her lightly on the nose. Ellie was surprised, but tried not to show it. She assumed this was some strange Andirovian custom.

"And this is our son, Prince John," growled the Emperor. He pushed forward a boy who was wearing an identical uniform, but no medals.

Ellie hesitated for a moment

wondering if she should kiss his nose, or shake his hand. She didn't fancy doing either. She wished he hadn't come.

Her mother nudged her and whispered firmly, "Say hello, Aurelia."

Ellie forced herself to smile, and held out her hand. "I'm delighted to meet you," she lied.

Prince John took her hand limply and gave it an unenthusiastic shake. "I'm really pleased to be here," he said, but his eyes suggested he didn't mean it.

"I'm sure you'll have such fun together," said the Queen, as she led them into the banqueting hall.

Ellie doubted it. She didn't like the look of Prince John at all. How was she going to survive a whole week with such a sulky, miserable boy and no ponies?

Chapter 4

The Queen took the Emperor's arm and led him to the banqueting hall. The King followed with the Empress, leaving Ellie to accompany Prince John. Fortunately there was no need to make polite conversation – the fanfare of trumpets was so loud that it was impossible to talk.

The banqueting hall glittered with crystal

A Puzzle for Princess Ellie

and silver. The other guests were already assembled, so the meal began as soon as they were settled in their seats. To Ellie's disappointment, hers was next to Prince John. She'd have to think of something to talk about.

"Did you enjoy your journey?" she asked, politely.

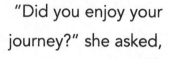

"No," snapped the Prince. "I was seasick."

"But you came by car." Prince John looked at her as if she were the stupidest person in the world. "Before we were in the car, we were on a ship," he explained. "I'm always sick on ships."

"Oh," said Ellie, wondering what to say next. A discussion on being sick didn't seem the best idea to accompany a meal. Fortunately the food arrived at that point and for once, Ellie was pleased Miss Stringle had taught her not to speak with her mouth full. By eating very slowly and taking several extra helpings, she managed to keep it full for most of the rest of the meal.

To her relief, Prince John left the table as soon as he had finished his strawberry meringue. "I must go to bed," he said. "It's been such a long day."

Ellie suspected he just wanted to miss the boring speeches, but she didn't argue. She was far too pleased to see him go. It let her off having to make polite conversation with him.

A Puzzle for Princess Ellie

There was no such escape the next morning. Prince John was in the sun lounge waiting for her when she came downstairs. He had abandoned his uniform for a shirt and tie, and replaced his naval hat with his everyday crown. But he still looked as bored as he had the night before.

"What would you like to do today?" she asked.

"What's on offer?" he replied with a shrug. He ran his finger round the inside of his shirt collar, trying to pull it away from his neck.

For the first time, Ellie felt a twinge of sympathy for him. He looked as uncomfortable in his clothes as she felt in her stiff white blouse and tartan skirt. Maybe, like her, he'd prefer to be wearing jeans and a T-shirt.

The Pony-Mad Princess

"There's chess," she suggested.

"That's boring," he sneered.

"Or ludo?"

"Too childish."

"How about snakes and ladders?" said Ellie, impatiently. Her sympathy had vanished as quickly as it had arrived.

Prince John waved his hand towards the window. "Can't we do something outside?" he asked.

Ellie immediately thought of riding. But she reluctantly pushed the idea away and suggested croquet instead.

A Puzzle for Princess Ellie

The Prince agreed without enthusiasm. He played with even less. Ellie knew knocking balls through hoops wasn't the most exciting activity in the world, but she had never before met anyone who seemed so bored by it. Halfway through the game, he stopped playing and started staring at the surrounding countryside instead.

Desperate for something to talk about, Ellie tried to catch his interest by telling him more about the palace. "We have a lovely stream through the grounds," she said.

"We have a river through ours," said the Prince.

Ellie sensed a competition developing. "Our palace has a hundred and eighty-two rooms," she said.

"Ours has four hundred and fifty," Prince

John replied, immediately.

"We have our own private beach," said Ellie, firmly. She was sure he couldn't beat that.

"Only one?" said Prince John in a mocking voice. "We have five kilometres of private coastline and our own marina."

Ellie's mind raced. There must be something here that was better than Andirovia. Suddenly, she remembered her last ride with Kate. "We've got a haunted wood," she said, triumphantly.

Chapter 5

To Ellie's delight, the Prince was lost for words. Now it was her turn to mock. "Don't tell me you haven't got any ghosts in Andirovia?" she said.

Prince John looked flustered. "Not that I know of," he admitted, reluctantly. He obviously wasn't used to losing. Then he thought for a moment and added, "But of course, I don't believe ghosts really exist."

At that moment, Kate's gran arrived
in her best cook's uniform and bobbed
a curtsey to the Prince.
"I thought you two might
be feeling peckish," she
said, putting down a tray
of lemonade and fruitcake
on a garden table.

A Puzzle for Princess Ellie

"Thanks," said Ellie. "We were just talking about ghosts."

Kate's gran shook her head. "I don't believe in them things," she said. "All that oohing and aahing and frightening people. When I'm dead, I'm sure I'll have better things to do with my time."

As she bustled away, John said, "You see. She doesn't believe in them either. I bet your wood's not haunted at all."

"Yes, it is," argued Ellie. "There's definitely something there. My friend Kate thinks it's the ghost of someone who grew trees. She calls him Archduke Edgar."

John gulped down a chunk of fruitcake and continued the argument.

"That's stupid," he said. "Archdukes don't do gardening. They lead armies and fight battles and stuff like that."

"Maybe this one didn't," said Ellie.

"You don't get to be a ghost by planting seeds," said John. "Everyone knows you have to die in some interesting way."

Ellie crossed her arms and stared at him. "So you admit ghosts exist then," she said, unable to keep the superiority out of her voice.

The Prince stared back defiantly. "Not yet," he said. "But tell me more about this wood. Did anything interesting ever happen there?"

"That's what I'm planning to find out," explained Ellie. "Do you want to help?"

Prince John shrugged. "I suppose so.

A Puzzle for Princess Ellie

Anything's better than croquet."

"We've got loads of history books," declared Ellie. "Some of them might mention the wood."

They drank the last of the lemonade and headed for the palace library. It was an enormous room with a high ceiling and shelves stacked with leather-bound books. Each one was stamped with a golden crown.

The Prince looked around in dismay. "How are we supposed to find what we want?"

Ellie wasn't sure. She'd been daydreaming about show jumping when Miss

Stringle had taught her about library classification. She knew even less about it than she did about spoons. "Perhaps we just start looking," she said, without much enthusiasm.

"I'm not reading all those books," declared Prince John. "It would be much better to look on the Internet. You have got a computer, haven't you?"

"Of course I have," Ellie snapped back. "It's in my room."

"Let's go then," said John, as he urged her out of the library. "We can play some computer games too. They're much better than stupid croquet."

Ellie sighed. She hoped he wouldn't think her room was stupid too. As they climbed the stairs, she tried to prepare him for its overwhelming pinkness. "It's Dad's fault," she explained. "He thinks all princesses like pink but *I* don't."

To her surprise, John was sympathetic. "My father's like that too. He thinks all princes like boats, but I hate them. I get seasick too easily."

His reaction filled Ellie with confidence. If he understood the problem, he might not make fun of her. She threw open her bedroom door and waved him in. "The computer's by the window," she said.

Prince John stepped inside and stared around the room in surprise. Then he burst out laughing.

Chapter 6

Ellie glared at John. "I told you it was pink," she said, angrily.

"But you didn't tell me about the ponies," he replied.

Ellie looked round the room and saw what he meant. She had been so worried about the pinkness that she'd forgotten about everything else. Pony posters covered the pink walls, pony books crammed the pink bookcases, and model ponies stood on every available surface.

She stared at him defiantly. "Don't you dare make fun of me," she shouted. "I just like ponies. There's nothing wrong with that."

"I know there's not," said John, with a huge smile that lit up his normally miserable face. "I'm not laughing at *you*."

"Then what's so funny?" said Ellie. She had calmed down a little, but she was still suspicious.

"Nothing," said John. "I'm just laughing because I'm happy. I've finally met someone who likes ponies as much as I do."

Ellie stared at him in astonishment. "So you like them too?" she asked.

"More than anything," said John. "I'd have told you before, but my father ordered me not to talk about ponies while I'm here. He thought it would bore you as much as it bores him."

A Puzzle for Princess Ellie

It was Ellie's turn to laugh now. "He was certainly wrong about that. But my dad's just as bad. He said I mustn't ride, or go to the stables, or mess about with my ponies. I'm supposed to give you all my attention."

John walked across the room and stared thoughtfully out of the window. Then he turned and grinned at Ellie. "I'm supposed to be polite to you. My father was very insistent about that. So now you've started talking about ponies, perhaps I'd better join in. It would be very rude if I didn't."

"That's brilliant," cried Ellie. "And if you want to go to the stables, I must go with you. I wouldn't be giving you my full attention if I didn't."

"Then what are we waiting for?" said John, as he headed for the door.

The Pony-Mad Princess

Although they had convinced themselves that they weren't breaking any rules, they didn't want to take any unnecessary risks. They checked carefully that no one was looking before they headed for the stables.

Meg was surprised to see them. "I thought you weren't allowed to come here for a few days," she said to Ellie.

After she had reassured Meg that everything was fine, Ellie introduced her to John. Then she took him to meet Shadow, Rainbow, Moonbeam, and Sundance, while he told her about the two chestnut mares he had left behind in Andirovia. Ellie noticed he had fewer ponies than her, but she didn't gloat about it. They were friends now, not competitors.

"Can we do anything to help?" Ellie asked Meg.

"I haven't groomed Rainbow and Sundance yet," said Meg. She paused and raised her eyebrows as she looked at their clothes. "But neither of you look dressed for stable work."

"Oh, that doesn't matter," said Ellie. She turned to John and asked, "Do you fancy doing some grooming?"

"Yes," said John, enthusiastically. Then he looked embarrassed and added, "But I don't know how. The servants always do it for me at home."

The Pony-Mad Princess

Ellie knew exactly how he felt. She had never been allowed to look after her ponies until Meg came. "Don't worry," she said. "I'll show you what to do."

She fetched the grooming kit from the tack room and tied up the two  ponies in the sunshine. Then she showed John how to use the different brushes and the hoof pick. It felt good to be the knowledgeable one of the pair. He certainly didn't think she was stupid any more.

Half an hour later, they stepped back and admired the results of their work with satisfaction. Both ponies were spotlessly clean. Their coats gleamed, their tails hung straight and untangled, and their hooves shone with hoof oil.

"I'd love to go for a ride on this one," said John, as he stroked Sundance's nose. The chestnut pony whickered with pleasure. Then he rubbed the side of his head on the Prince's shoulder so hard that he nearly pushed him over.

Ellie grinned mischievously. "If you want to ride, it's obviously my duty to go with you." She paused and looked down at her skirt. "I'll have to get changed first. Do you need to borrow some clothes? I'm afraid everything's pink, even my spare hard hat."

"I don't care," said John. "I'll wear anything if it means I can ride."

"Let's go then," said Ellie. "The sooner we're changed, the sooner we can get back."

They were in such a hurry that they forgot to check if anyone was around. They raced out of the yard and bumped straight into the Emperor of Andirovia.

Chapter 7

To Ellie's horror, the Emperor was not alone. The King was beside him, and the Queen and the Empress were close behind. All four of them were staring at Ellie and John in dismay.

"You are filthy!" yelled the Emperor, pointing at John in disgust.

"So are you, Aurelia," added the Queen.

The Pony-Mad Princess

Ellie looked down at herself and saw they were right. Her hands were caked with dirt and grease, her legs and skirt were dusty and her blouse was no longer white. John looked even worse. He had spilled hoof oil down his trousers and, in his attempts to wipe it off, he had got it on his hands and wiped it on his nose.

A Puzzle for Princess Ellie

The Empress walked up to him and sniffed suspiciously. "You smell of horse," she said in an accusing voice.

"What have you been doing, Aurelia?" shouted the King. "I distinctly forbade you to go to the stables."

Ellie bit her lip nervously as she looked at their angry faces. If she couldn't talk her way out of this, she was in big trouble. "But John wanted to see the ponies and you told me to entertain him."

"Ponies, ponies, ponies," shouted the Emperor. He glowered at John in frustration. "I told you not to talk about them while you're here."

John pulled a suitably apologetic face. "Princess Aurelia started talking about them first," he said in a very polite voice. "It would have been rude not to reply."

The Emperor turned to the King in surprise. "Is your child as pony-mad as mine?" he asked.

The King sighed. "She's probably even madder," he said. "And it's so hard to live with."

The two rulers started commiserating with each other on the problems of parenthood. They seemed to have completely lost interest in their children.

Ellie sidled up to her mother. "Can we go now?" she whispered. "We want to have a ride."

"You can go and get clean," said the Queen, firmly. "You are both having lunch with us and after that the Prime Minister has promised to entertain John with some conjuring."

"But what about our ride?" said Ellie.

A Puzzle for Princess Ellie

Magic tricks sounded a poor substitute for ponies.

John looked pleadingly at his mother with big, wide eyes. "Please, Mama," he said.

Ellie was impressed. She wished she could put on such an innocent expression whenever she wanted. It would be really useful when she was in trouble.

John's big eyes obviously worked. The Empress smiled. "Maybe they could go later," she suggested to the Queen. After much looking at watches, the two mothers agreed that riding at four was a reasonable idea.

"That's ages away," groaned John as he walked back to the palace with Ellie.

"But going later means Kate can come with us," said Ellie. "We can go right up to the top of the hill and show you the view."

"I've got a much better idea," said John. "Let's go to the haunted wood and try to find the ghost."

Ellie's eyes lit up with excitement. Was there a chance that they could really solve the puzzle?

Ellie showered as quickly as she could in her en-suite bathroom. She had just finished dressing when John tapped on her bedroom door.

A Puzzle for Princess Ellie

"There's just time to look up ghost hunting before lunch," he said, as he walked over to the computer. There were dozens of useful websites and they soon had a list of everything they needed to track down a ghost.

"We'd better take headcollars too," said Ellie. "We might need to tie the ponies up."

"That's a good idea," said John. "I can

bring my camera, watch, and tape recorder. Can you find everything else?"

Ellie nodded as she looked down at the paper in her hand. It was such a curious list. She might have thought of backpacks and notebooks herself, but she would never have dreamed of taking talcum powder, a thermometer, and a set of wind chimes.

Hunting ghosts was more complicated than she'd expected. And what would they do if they found one?

Chapter 8

Lunch was even more elaborate than usual. A whole roast swan sat on the sideboard. Ellie eyed it warily and chose to eat cheese instead. She quite liked swans and preferred to see them swimming.

The meal dragged on and on and so did the conjuring display that followed it. The Prime Minister was not a brilliant magician.

Ellie could see how many of his tricks were done but she pretended that she couldn't.

She gasped with amazement when he produced an egg from behind her ear. She clapped loudly when he turned a bottle into a bunch of flowers, and she pretended

A Puzzle for Princess Ellie

not to notice that the
rabbit had chewed
a hole in his top
hat and escaped.

The hands on the ornate gold clock on
the mantelpiece moved frustratingly slowly.
It felt as if the performance was going on
for ever. But just before half past three, the
final trick was finished, and Ellie and John
were free to leave. There was just time to
gather all the equipment together and get
changed before their ride.

Kate was waiting for them in the yard.
She was clutching the message they had
sent her and was looking very excited. "I've
brought these just in case," she said,
holding out three garlic bulbs.

"In case of what?" asked John. "Garlic's

for keeping vampires away, not ghosts."

Kate thrust the garlic back in her pocket. "I'll take them anyway. They might be useful."

Ellie showed John how to put the saddle and bridle on Sundance while Kate got Rainbow and Moonbeam ready. Then they stuffed the ponies' headcollars in their backpacks, mounted their ponies and clattered out of the yard.

Rainbow was frisky. She tossed her head and tried to trot. Ellie had to keep a firm hold on the reins to keep her walking. She wanted to give John time to get used to Sundance before they tried going any faster.

She needn't have worried. The chestnut pony was as well-behaved as usual, and John was obviously a good rider.

They turned off the drive into a meadow.

A Puzzle for Princess Ellie

Rainbow started to jog as soon as she felt the grass under her feet. Ellie battled to make the grey pony walk again, but a sudden commotion to one side took her attention. Moonbeam was so excited that she'd lifted her back legs off the ground in a huge buck.

"Eeek!" said Kate as she struggled to stay in the saddle. "These ponies have too much energy."

"Let's use some of it up," said Ellie. She glanced over to John. "Are you okay to go faster?"

John grinned. "I'm ready when you are."

Ellie stopped fighting Rainbow and let her trot properly. The others followed her lead around the edge of the field.

When they reached the top, they slowed to a walk to go through a gate. It led them onto a stretch of open parkland. It was the perfect place for a gallop.

Ellie squeezed slightly with her legs and Rainbow leaped forward eagerly. Soon she was racing side by side with Sundance and Moonbeam, as they galloped across the grass.

Ellie leaned forward, urging Rainbow on. It was wonderful to be riding again. She would have happily galloped for ever. But eventually she felt Rainbow starting to tire. She let her slow to a canter, then a trot, and finally to a walk.

The gallop had used up the ponies' surplus energy. They were all much better behaved. Rainbow was content to walk now so Ellie lengthened the reins to let her stretch her neck and relax.

A Puzzle for Princess Ellie

They rode further and further from the palace until they found the gate Ellie and Kate had gone through before. They walked along the edge of the cornfield and turned right when they reached the high wall. Ellie felt a shiver of excitement when she saw the haunted wood in front of them.

She stopped Rainbow at the entrance. The path ahead looked even darker and more mysterious than it had before.

She looked at John. "This was your idea. What do we do now?"

"We'd better get organized," he replied. He switched on the tape recorder in his pocket, clipped a microphone to his collar, and said in a serious voice, "Time 4.46 pm. Temperature?" He looked questioningly at Kate.

Kate stared back at him. "The thermometer's in my backpack. I can't use it while I'm riding."

John shrugged and started again. "Time: 4.47 pm. Temperature: quite hot. We are just entering the haunted wood."

Ellie made Rainbow walk on. The grey pony snorted suspiciously as she stepped into the dark tunnel made by the trees. Her ears were pricked forward, alert for danger.

A Puzzle for Princess Ellie

They moved forward quietly. The ponies' hooves made almost no sound on the layer of dead leaves covering the ground. Ellie glanced nervously from side to side, expecting something to jump out at her at any moment.

Suddenly, the silence was broken by John. "Time: 5.02. We are now inside the wood. The temperature is noticeably lower."

Ellie shivered. He was right. It was chilly. Was that because the trees cut out the sun, or was there some other reason? Was it the ghost making the air so cold?

Chapter 9

The path led them deeper and deeper into the wood. Suddenly Ellie realized they were nearly at the place where Rainbow had been spooked on their last ride. She leaned forward and gave the pony a reassuring pat. "There's nothing to be scared of," she said, as confidently as she could. But she kept a firm hold on the reins just in case.

A Puzzle for Princess Ellie

Rainbow walked forward steadily, each step bringing her closer to that mysterious place. Ellie started to relax. "Maybe the ghost isn't here today," she said.

She spoke too soon. Rainbow suddenly stopped dead and whirled round to the right. "Steady, girl," said Ellie, as she stopped her and turned her to face forward again. "There's nothing there." She pushed the pony on with her legs and felt her start to step forward.

Just as Ellie thought the trouble was over, Rainbow changed direction in mid-step and spun round to the left. This time Ellie was caught off balance. She lost both stirrups and slid sideways in the saddle.

"Steady," she called again, but the pony was too frightened to listen. She whirled once more and Ellie slipped over Rainbow's shoulder.

"Ouch!" she cried, as she landed in a patch of brambles, still holding tightly to the reins.

"Time: 5.14," said John into his tape recorder. "Rainbow has seen something. Is it the ghost?"

Kate jumped down from Moonbeam's back and helped free Ellie from the prickly stems. "What shall we do now?" she asked.

Ellie stroked Rainbow gently. "It's all right,"

she whispered in a soothing voice. "You don't have to go any further." Then she turned to the others and announced, "We'll have to hunt on foot now. It's not fair to make her go on when she's so frightened."

"Let's tie the ponies up here," said John.

"No," said Ellie. "They need to be further away so they won't be scared." She led Rainbow back along the path until the grey pony seemed more relaxed. "This will do," she said, as she tied her up with the headcollar from her backpack. "Rainbow shouldn't be frightened here."

Kate and John joined her and pulled the headcollars from their backpacks. Soon, all three ponies were tied up side by side. Sundance immediately started to doze. Even Rainbow and Moonbeam looked reasonably calm.

When the ponies were settled, John took charge. "I'll take the camera," he said. "You take the wind chime, Kate. You can hang it over there in that tree."

"Why?" asked Kate, who hadn't read any of the websites.

"It's to spot any movement in the air," explained John. Then he handed Ellie the talcum powder. "I want you to sprinkle that all over the ground. It'll help show up any ghostly footprints."

Ellie walked nervously along the path, glancing from side to side and ready to run at any moment. When she was sure she was past whatever Rainbow had seen, she stopped and walked backwards towards John, sprinkling powder on the path as she went.

A Puzzle for Princess Ellie

Halfway along she was joined by Kate who had just finished tying up the wind chimes.

"Do you want this?" said Kate, as she pressed something into Ellie's spare hand. Her voice was edged with fear.

Ellie stopped sprinkling the powder for a moment and looked down to see what she was holding. It was the garlic.

"I know John said it won't help, but he might be wrong," Kate whispered.

"Thanks," said Ellie. She clutched the garlic tightly. The feel of it was comforting.

"Time: 5.41," said John into his tape recorder. "Everything is prepared. We are now waiting for something to happen."

"Let's wait over there," said Ellie, pointing at a fallen log close to the path.

The others agreed but, on the way, John stopped dramatically and pointed at the ground.

"Time: 5.44," he said. "We see a footprint in the powder."

Ellie's heart missed a beat as she stared at the path. John was right. There was a footprint. Was it the ghost?

John pulled out a magnifying glass and stared through it at the footprint. "Mmm,"

he said. "It's not very big. Maybe it's the ghost of a child." He paused again and added, "A child wearing boots."

Kate coughed gently and looked embarrassed. "I think it might be me," she said. She stepped forward and put her foot gently into the print. It fitted exactly. "I'm ever so sorry. I thought I'd managed not to step in the powder."

"Time: 5.48," said John. "A false alarm."

Ellie breathed a sigh of relief. Although the idea of hunting ghosts had sounded like fun, she wasn't at all sure she wanted to find one. She sat down on the log hoping fervently that nothing else would happen.

For a few minutes, nothing did. They sat together waiting. Suddenly, a tinkling sound broke the silence. It was the wind chime, but there wasn't any wind.

Chapter 10

"What was that?" cried Ellie, as she leaped to her feet. She tightened her grip on the garlic just in case.

"Perhaps it's the ghost," said John. For the first time, there was a trace of fear in his voice. He seemed to have forgotten about the tape recorder.

The wind chimes tinkled again. This time

A Puzzle for Princess Ellie

Ellie was looking at them. She saw the leaves above them move as well. "There's something in the tree," she said.

"Is it the ghost?" whispered Kate in a frightened voice. She ducked down behind the log as if she hoped it would protect her.

The leaves moved again, and Ellie saw a flash of chestnut fur between them. A red squirrel bounded into sight. It sat on the branch for a moment before scampering away up the trunk of the tree.

"Phew," said Ellie in relief. "I've never been so pleased to see a squirrel."

"Me too," said Kate. She stood up, brushing dead leaves and earth from her jodhpurs.

John took a deep breath and looked puzzled. "Can you smell something?" he asked.

Ellie sniffed the air. There definitely was a smell, but she couldn't work out what it was. "Where's it coming from?" she asked.

The three of them spread out with their noses in the air as they tried to sniff out the source. The smell faded if they walked back towards the ponies. It faded if they went further along the path, and it faded if they turned right and walked in among the trees. It only grew stronger if they walked near the wall.

A Puzzle for Princess Ellie

"There must be something behind there," said Ellie, pointing at the bricks.

"It's not the ghost, is it?" said Kate, nervously. "Ghosts don't smell, do they?"

"Some of them do," said John. "Lots of haunted places have strange smells."

"And so do lots of non-haunted ones," said Ellie, as much to reassure herself as anyone else.

The only way to find the truth was to look on the other side of the wall. But it was much too hard to climb.

"Look over there!" shouted John, pointing to a nearby tree. "If we climb that we should be able to swing over onto the top of the wall."

Ellie looked up at the branches in dismay. She had never climbed a tree before and wasn't sure how to start.

Kate must have guessed her problem. "It's not hard," she said. "You just grab hold of this branch, put one foot on this bump, and then the other on that one."

As she spoke, she swarmed up the tree like a monkey. She made climbing look easy.

Ellie found it wasn't. She had three tries before she managed to grab the branch.

A Puzzle for Princess Ellie

Then her feet slithered on the slippery bark as she tried to heave herself up the trunk. She only managed it in the end because John gave her a shove from underneath. Then he followed her up.

Kate was waiting for them impatiently. "The next bit's even easier," she said. "I've found three strong branches that reach the wall. We can take one each and wriggle along them."

Ellie looked at the branches and at the ground beneath them. It was a long way to fall. For a brief moment, she wondered if she should stay where she was and let the others go on without her. Then her curiosity overcame her fear. She wanted to see for herself what was hiding on the other side of that wall.

The Pony-Mad Princess

She wriggled onto the middle branch and, trying hard not to look down, she started to edge her way along. Kate and John made their way along the other two branches, and they all reached the wall at the same time.

A Puzzle for Princess Ellie

Together they peered down, straight into a pair of eyes. Something was looking up at them from the other side. But it wasn't a ghost. It was an enormous pig.

Kate pointed at it in delight. "That explains the smell," she said.

"But it doesn't explain the ghost," said John.

"Yes, it does," laughed Ellie. "It says in one of my books that lots of ponies are frightened of pigs. Rainbow must be one of them. She didn't see a ghost at all. She smelled the pig."

"So there's no ghostly gardener," said Kate.

"And no haunted wood," said John.

Neither of them sounded very disappointed. Ellie suspected they were

as relieved as she was. The ghost hunt had
been quite scary enough without finding
a ghost.

"But there is an Archduke Edgar," said
John. He stood to attention on top of the
wall and saluted the pig. "I bring you
greetings from Andirovia, Your Royal
Highness," he said with a broad grin.

Then Ellie and her friends collapsed
with laughter.

For more sparkly adventures of

The Pony-Mad Princess

look out for

Princess Ellie's Starlight Adventure

Princess Ellie's Starlight Adventure

Chapter 1

"Princess Aurelia!" The shout echoed down the palace corridor.

Princess Ellie groaned. She was on her way to the stables and didn't want to stop. She didn't want to be called by her real name either. She much preferred Ellie.

The owner of the voice rushed up. It was a maid who looked very flustered and out of breath. "You'd better come quickly, Your Highness. The King and Queen are very cross."

Ellie followed the maid back along the corridor, wondering what she'd done wrong this time. For once, she couldn't think of anything. She had been very polite for the last few days and it was ages since she'd last turned up for dinner in her jodhpurs, or muddy boots.

The King and Queen were waiting impatiently for her in their favourite part of the royal garden. Their arms were crossed and their faces looked even angrier than Ellie had expected.

"Look at the mess you've made, Aurelia," roared the King, as he pointed at the grass. The normally smooth, green surface of the lawn was pockmarked with hoofprints.

"How dare you ride in my garden," wailed the Queen. She sniffed angrily and dabbed away a tear with a handkerchief embroidered with silver crowns.

"It wasn't me," said Ellie, indignantly.

"Don't tell lies," snapped the King.

Ellie resisted the temptation to snap back. She knew from experience that it would only make matters worse. "I *am* telling the truth," she insisted, as calmly as possible. "I've got all the palace grounds to ride in. I don't need to use the lawn."

"Hmm," said the Queen, thoughtfully. "Aurelia does have a point, my dear."

The King was less convinced. He stared suspiciously at Ellie and asked, "How do you explain the hoofprints then?"

Ellie bent down and ran her fingers round one of the holes in the grass, while she tried to think of an explanation. Meg, the royal groom, had a horse of her own, but she was far too sensible to ride Gipsy in the garden.

Ellie's four ponies were the only other suspects. There weren't any others at the palace.

"If you haven't ridden here, who has?" asked the Queen. "It certainly wasn't Kate."

Ellie didn't need reminding about that. She had been lonely since her best friend had gone to visit her father, who was building a road in some distant desert. Life was much more exciting and fun when Kate was staying with her gran, the palace cook. They spent all their time together, riding Ellie's ponies, or helping out at the stables. Once, they had even saved Sundance's life after he got out of his stable in a storm.

That memory gave Ellie a flash of inspiration. "One of the ponies must have escaped," she announced.

"That's a possibility," admitted the Queen.

"But we can't have ponies running all over the place doing whatever they please."

"Definitely not," said the King, firmly. "Tell Meg to make sure it doesn't happen again."

Ellie promised that she would. Then she ran to the yard to check which of her ponies was missing. To her surprise, none of them were. Moonbeam, Rainbow, Sundance, and Shadow were all in their stables, happily munching hay. So was Gipsy.

"That's really strange," said Meg, when she heard what had happened.

"Perhaps one of them escaped and then came back," suggested Ellie. "Sundance knows how to undo bolts."

"He must have learned how to do them up as well," replied Meg. "His door was definitely fastened this morning." She looked at Ellie's anxious face and smiled. "Don't worry. I'll double check everything tonight before I go to bed and I'll put a special clip on Sundance's door so he can't undo it."

"That should stop it happening again," said Ellie, confidently. If there was no way her ponies could escape, there was no way they could do any damage. By the morning, her parents would probably have forgotten all about the mysterious hoofprints.

Unfortunately, Ellie was wrong. Before she'd had time for breakfast, she was summoned to the garden again and so was Meg. Ellie's parents were even angrier than before. The King's face was nearly as red as the ruby in his everyday crown.

"Look at this. There are even more

hoofprints than yesterday," said the King, as he stared at them both accusingly.

"And my prize petunias are ruined," added the Queen, holding up a mangled plant. "Your wretched ponies have been eating my flowers."

"They can't have," said Ellie.

"They *must* have," snapped the King

"Excuse me, Your Majesties," said Meg, politely. "The ponies were all shut securely in their stables when I went to bed last night, and they were still there this morning."

"Then they must have been out in between," said the Queen. "It's the only possible explanation. They are the only ponies at the palace."

The King glared at Meg. "This is *your* fault. Go back to the stables and make sure it doesn't happen again. If it does, we may have to consider your position."

Ellie gasped with horror as they walked away, "You can't sack her. She hasn't done anything wrong."

"Are you admitting that you have then?" said her father, seriously. "Were you lying about not riding here?"

"No," said Ellie. "But…"

"There are no buts about it," said the King before she had time to finish. "It's Meg's job to keep the ponies under control. If she can't do that, I'm afraid she must go."

To find out what happens next read

Princess Ellie's Starlight Adventure

The Pony-Mad Princess

Collect all the sparkly adventures of Princess Ellie and her friends.

Princess Ellie to the Rescue

Can Ellie save her beloved pony, Sundance, when he goes missing?

ISBN: 0 7460 6018 1

Princess Ellie's Starlight Adventure

When strange hoofprints appear on the palace lawn Ellie has to find the culprit.

ISBN: 0 7460 6021 1

Princess Ellie's Secret

Ellie comes up with a secret plan to stop her first ever pony, Shadow, from being sold.

ISBN: 0 7460 6019 X

Princess Ellie's Moonlight Mystery

Ellie and Kate are enjoying pony camp, until they hear mysterious noises in the night.

ISBN: 0 7460 6022 X

A Puzzle for Princess Ellie

Ellie has to solve the puzzle of why Rainbow won't go down the spooky woodland path.

ISBN: 0 7460 6020 3

A Surprise for Princess Ellie

Ellie and her friends set off in search of adventure, and end up with a big surprise!

ISBN: 0 7460 6023 8

All books are priced at £3.99